Nadia was born on a first day of the year in Morocco. She grew up in Granada, one beautiful town located in the southern coast of Spain, where studied a short course of chemistry. At her 30 years of age, she travelled to London, UK, where she stayed until 2022. There, she studied various short courses of administration and accountancy. She has worked as a pharmacy technician at King's College Hospital for over four years, there she also obtained the qualification of the same title.

Now, she lives in a little but absolutely adorable town of Malta named Marsaskala.

Nadia is a new, promising and passionate writer. Although this is her first publication, she has written innumerable proses and short stories whilst growing up; she still does. Now she is totally focused in her new career as a writer that has always been her passion.

To my greatest ever dear mum, who, despite her prompt party off this physical world, always has been at my side, and even from where she is, she is still with me—all the time.

Mum, there are no words to thank you for all you have taught and given to me in so little time and beyond the clouds that separate us and for guiding my way.

Because you will always be in me,

Because I will always be you,

This is the best I have, and this is just for you.

Nadia Aparicio

DROPS OF LIGHT AND DARK

Some Little Things That Would Not Let You Sleep Without Some Thinking…

AUSTIN MACAULEY PUBLISHERS™
LONDON · CAMBRIDGE · NEW YORK · SHARJAH

Copyright © Nadia Aparicio 2024

The right of Nadia Aparicio to be identified as author of this work has been asserted by the author in accordance with sections 77 and 78 of the Copyright, Designs and Patents Act 1988.

All rights reserved. No part of this publication may be reproduced, stored in a retrieval system, or transmitted in any form or by any means, electronic, mechanical, photocopying, recording, or otherwise, without the prior permission of the publishers.

Any person who commits any unauthorised act in relation to this publication may be liable to criminal prosecution and civil claims for damages.

This is a work of fiction. Names, characters, businesses, places, events, locales, and incidents are either the products of the author's imagination or used in a fictitious manner. Any resemblance to actual persons, living or dead, or actual events is purely coincidental.

A CIP catalogue record for this title is available from the British Library.

ISBN 9781398441729 (Paperback)
ISBN 9781398441736 (ePub e-book)

www.austinmacauley.com

First Published 2024
Austin Macauley Publishers Ltd®
1 Canada Square
Canary Wharf
London
E14 5AA

To all those souls that have been with me all the way, suffering with me, guiding me and teaching me.

To all those souls that ever felt compelled to correct me on my way to heaven or hell.

To all those souls that I have recently met, because they have also helped me to get up on my feet once more, and they showed me that looking at life from an even soil is just what a fearless, valiant soul does...

To Darren, Sal, Dwayne, Wayne and Steve, because they have supported me, un-tiredly. They have been so patient with me and taught me so many important things in life as well as how to be a good pharmacy technician.

To Margaret Rose, whom I love to call Marga because I feel her so close, the forever admin manager who has always, always been so much more to every person ever passing by her way, I am certain she holds all the magic I will talk about later on, in this very book, because she made me see I am important too, to Louise, to Matt T and Matt F, to many other colleagues at King's College Hospital, to my teachers at Westminster Kingsway College, Aisar, Stephen, Shagufta and other teacher supporters, to all those friends in London that were as quick and fast in appearing as in to disappearing because they taught me how long it takes to see the actual blossom of a relationship. Many thanks to all. I will never forget.

Dear Stardust

I want to swim in the ocean. I want to have my chance to breathe under the waters that bathe the shores of every dream come true.

May it be when the soul flies into those eyes, may it be when the white sun grits the beautiful moon, maybe when we're born together, each day, each immense dawn, and each breath we take...

So, maybe tomorrow, I'll find my way home...

Meanwhile, I stop, I analyse, and it is just unbelievable the number of names and phone numbers that occupy the memory of the dumb device I absolutely always carry on, just to not to feel naked, dowdy, neglected just not to feel apart from the rest of the world , or disconnected.

So much memory that serves nothing...

Tonight, there will be more candles, for me, for all those little beasts close to me then, and far now lost, for all times, for all the souls I have seen passing by me... and I don't even remember, and I cannot even name...

So much memory... for nothing...

So many steps, in circles, so much walking... only to stop feeling that anguish... only to go back to the same dark room... only to light that barely companionable incense...

To have an infinite power, the infinite power that enables you to call the world yours… to sleep in the clouds, to dream in the soul, to live in the universe… because in the end, we are just dust. In the end as well as in the beginning, we are all that stardust. We are magic, the so forgotten magic, so idealised, that we forget what we carry it in our very insides…

So much memory… for nothing…

So, so much heart that it hurts, even the happiness hurts and, all of a sudden, we live. We are alive with sensations, glances, moments, feelings without name, without a name but filled with so much sense that ends up filling a whole entire life that was before completely empty of wings, of new glares, of flying thoughts, so little thoughts… so many thoughts…

And all of a sudden, so much memory to serve nothing converted in: 'if with one sole grain of sand can I build my perfect beach…'

So much memory… that serves nothing?

Many times, we forget what magic is; magic is when we empty our feelings into another soul. Magic is when we open our eyes to look with the pureness we didn't know we had, magic to open the eyes and believe is what we need to support our own ethereal being.

So, so much that truly, in the end nothing is left with us… nothing…

So, so much given, and forever lost considered, so much that one day we may be reborn… into a different but equally miraculous little shell…

We only fear because we do not know how to fill the empty glass…

Most probingly, so much memory turns into pain every time something falls…

We want to fly but we break our own wings. We want to shout but we implode, cracking our own voices instead. We simply forget, the magical power we own as the most unbelievable birth right, that power we hold in our naked, naïve hands...

And so much memory... is converted into so little...

And we wish to become all that we once were, but we did not want, we did not want to accept...

The raw truth is that I know nobody, nobody, only just I get to know my own thoughts, those that resemble some lost clouds, so far from me, in that faraway sky... I can only touch, skim, barely feel my body, and that is not nearly enough... and the thirst remains with me.

So many dark, confusing dreams... that I keep lighting candles as if they were to light my path, through and after the angles of that staircase of my life, obscure and clandestine...

So many wings, and so much magic... maybe condemned to get to be nothing... so much magic, so many wings... utterly useless until someone comes to remind us. We need a little push, a tender, sincere hand... To remind us that we are and will still be islands until we do not build a bridge, to remind us that dreams are not to be drowned alone, on our own, so, so much that it is difficult to name it all.

But the truth is so much different... The real truth comes when we close our eyes and look. It is only then when the power of the soul awakes, and the stretch cage of this body and the grandness of it becomes the way, the path... and the grand truth of this beautiful life...

So much deceit, so much truth... so much life... so much desire to live it the wildest way possible, so much will, so endless... so much life...

Despite all the effort that takes to mature one's heart, I would gladly remain in the sweetest of the childhoods. I would gladly remain in the pureness of knowing, the pureness of not judging, not give opinion, but to simply accept, to simply see, to simply live…

Despite all the effort that takes, being a legend every day, to keep holding the magic in the naked hands that one day saw me coming into this world and are still with me, guiding, dressing and feeding me, even today…

> Despite all, I'll never forget I am stardust,
> And into stardust I will convert once again,
> But by now, I want to keep holding the magic
> With these hands dressed of flesh
> And a fine layer of stardust makeup.

Awww... But the Pen and Paper...

I thought I was feeling like writing... It's now a little while ago I didn't do it; the raw need showed up again finally. That infinite edge of edged feelings... somewhat jumbled, mixed, also... soft. With a little touch of consciousness, and a vague sensation of reality, brought by a little something... magical...

Although present, everything getting to my inners seems to be like a movie... distant, already passed or yet to be, just anxiously formed by my greedy, inpatient brain, with the unconditional help of my so told grown, old soul... that never, ever rests in peace because there is always something, something to analyse, to study, to feel, to record, to make sure I very well get the feeling of. I personally believe these awful persistent clouds have made their way into my poor, already-wounded heart, and then straight into my soul, also already quite tired. Even a warrior can get tired. I could write a book just and only with my tired feelings, my tiring experiences, my tiring life. Always driven just by the life itself, always wondering when the suffering will end and the joy commence.

I can feel my signal, my Morse code becoming weaker, late.

I don't want to believe it is becoming late for me to... live, to really grow, to get what I want in life, to move, to enjoy, to expand, to give, to gift, to take and so many more things to do in life.

*****

I wasn't even sure about how to bring alive this writing, whether in writing... writing or on e-writing. It seemed the turn for the e-writing to take place as it almost never does, but awww..., the pen and paper... the old, traditional pen and paper... nothing like it; nothing compared to the feeling of your hand moving, creating the ink trace through the white, unpolluted blank space just waiting for you to fill it in with new, unexpected adventures, full of extremely original connotations of all the spices that actually make your heart pump and take away your breath, with everything that keeps you alive...

Awww... the pen and paper... the relief... the everlasting friend, as dark as it may get and beyond, unconditional, clean, true, pure, unexpecting, undemanding, unconditional, true friend... to the end, the end of times...

Awww, but the pen and paper that have seen me grow my body from a certain beginning, to a certain consistency, to a certain doubt, to a certain resignation, and then... to another one of so, so many transformations, that I cannot even count; Aw... the pen and paper that have untiredly heard me complain about almost anything under the sun... the one that has accompanied me in my loneliest times, the pen and paper that has always been and always will be a part of my life, and most importantly, the greatest part of me...

Like the wild creatures of this world, as they feel the wind, the rain, the waves, they feel the north calling into their very core for them, and they release themselves into the widest horizon, into the wild world that gave them the strongest, purest, life-lasting and very based sense to be, to exist and fight through this madness, to find once more their purpose; and so they fly, they, somehow, always manage to emerge from the shit, as deep as it can ever get to be, as deep as it can hurt and last in their worn off souls, as deep as it can go into their thinking, way deeper past their skin and the meaning... of all the dreams. There is no sense to be without dreaming... There simply is no way to be without them, as dreams are the very connexion with the universe where we actually come from, where we realise... we exist...

There is simply so, so much more that needs to be given credit for...

And so you have to let your feelings and soul go for what they really are, what they really need, where they really need and want to be, where they really need to start over for the sake of your own mental health and wild condition preserving, never knowing where the wind is going to take them... but I'll sure go with it and land on my feet, to tell one day to my very, descending all the adventures, and ups and downs I had to go through in the past in order to meet them today, to get them into this fucked world to allow them to fix it at once, as I could not do so...

Awww, but the pen and paper...

The great challenge to free yourself into the emptiness and release the wild so long held in the guts that now shouts for something new and vibrant... to breathe fresh new air, under the sunlight and beyond the moon and the starts...

I'm gone now, for a better while for sure to be…
Thanks for all the support and the moaning too…
It all taught me as well as surely made me grow in a way,
I'll never forget.
I know how forgetful your world is,
But please try and remember me the way I will you…
Wildly and dearly.

The Lion Heart

I've read so many stories about lion hearts, many types of them...

But what is a lion heart? What is he made of? How does he move, how does he wake up in the morning or lie down to fall deep into dreams?

Who does he regard and who does he despises?

I have really read so many stories about lion hearts, and I have even watched films about so many of them disguised in many different characters, but always in possession of a great and big lion heart.

A lion heart always goes forward, even when it hurts, a lion heart, a real one, also cries, the bravest, in front of others too...

The true lion heart forgives, although never forgets, but in doing so, it also learns to stop forgiving and forgetting and starts holding people to their actions, even when that means holding its own heart to the pain the most loved ones held him to.

The true lion heart fights a pulse with the vivid horrors of some of his dreams, even the most scary ones, and wins.

A lion heart, when he forgives and forgets, keeps the worse and most cherished moments as treasures, equally valuable, he keeps them in the same room he keeps his lion heart.

But ahh… the lion heart can also fear, shed tears of blood. He can also doubt, and, sometimes, he is not even sure of what he's doing, where he is leading his steps; sometimes, many more times than is to believe, a lion heart crumbles down exhausted, short for belief and love for life and for others…

They also fall. Lion hearts also need help even when they do not let a sound leave their bodies, and they oblige themselves to keep going without pause and without a bearing, friendly hand.

But one thing is for sure, only they know how to really dream. They do not know how to retire and do not know when to cease. They know the best how to stand back up after falling, after the sorrow, after the lost battle. Only lion hearts know to charge back at the barbarous, ferocious and tremendously cold raid, indiscriminate, well enough to win the war, once and for all.

Only after the cold is gone do the lion hearts go back home, to finally rest on the luck and bravery that won the peace, the peace that brought them the power of powering themselves, on the hope and courage that lead them, the hope and the courage that made it possible for them to go back home full-handed with victory, full of the same simple, plain, but proud gaze they once left with.

A huge comeback, anyway or no coming back at all, also full of wounds, and perhaps some of them will never heal, some others not even in the skin anymore, but much deeper.

The huge come back, that a much more confident lion heart allows for himself, though perhaps never anyone will ever know how much more confident, how much more wounded, and how much prouder, which is precisely the result of the real and biggest lion heart inside them, the humblest heart of all.

I think, I may even be sure that I have seen that lion heart somewhere before, somewhere, quite close to me, somewhere very close to my own heart. A lion heart is never alone, never completely nor truly alone anyway.

And so, I have seen that glance, I have felt it in my eyes before, so many times actually that I myself have grown confident in it, grateful, comfortable and accustomed to its warmth, to its big odysseys right before getting to its real fairness, as much as with its own heart as with others.

I have seen, first-hand, I have woken up every morning with a lion heart, feeling its pure desperation, as also have a I felt the true courage that lives in the core of the lion heart, lift its spirits, once more, to fight, yet again, full of heart and full of the convincement, that one day, fight, there will be no more, no more sorrow, no more pain nor any doubt, one day, fight no more.

I believe that lion and that heart are not so apart from each other...

I've seen them in my dreams, them both, so close, to be one. In my dreams, I've seen their smile, and I've seen their sun...

I've seen a life I can live where my heart gets tan, warmed beyond imagination by the love of the beloved ones. I believe I've seen that place, in my life, where everyone and everything is even better than I could have ever imagined.

This is where the lion heart leads his steps; this is where he is headed.

A massive thanks to all that have battled with
As well as for me, and have never left me down.
I'll never forget.

The Untamed Universe Is Us

And thus, only the day we accept that nor the world and even less the universe belongs to us, but on the contrary it is us who belong to them. Only that day is when everything really starts in one's life. The salt in the sea dries the wounds of the soul. The sun heals the glance, cures the gestures, and so the love we thought we professed to ourselves. And we learn to love again.

Sometimes it is sad to realise who someday, seeming to be very long ago, we were, and what we became going through a life without sun, bare of kisses and confidant allies. Memories that fill the heart with people, feelings, moments; memories that fill the heart with wild desire...

Unfortunately, there are steps that cannot be undone; and that's not nice nor simple to accept because there are steps that deduct from us, instead of adding to our being; if I could really choose, most likely I would not choose to be any other person, but I would choose other reality, a different life, a very different fate.

Another, very different hearth to warm my heart and seed hope in my magic, to sing lullabies to my dreams instead of pushing the smiles with hurry, turning them into tears and hate.

A family, a home and a hearth that sings to the heart and takes it for a walk under the summer sun, bright shining light, a hearth that looks at me with a so-profound glare that makes me genuinely grow, form the inside, feeling secure, with the closest, unconditional nearness with confidence.

Like those thoughts that one never says (even though I have not very well defined that concept in my personality) like them remains today my glance, just drawn in my soul, hiding from everybody and everything else. Just because I am not really sure and, in fact, I fairly doubt any other soul would ever like any of the drawings in my broken, bored soul, that very poorly works without the sacred food that provide the sunshine and the blue, immense ocean, so fiercely dear to me.

Yet today, nothing seeds magic in my soul,
Nothing heals my poor glance,
Which is still drawn in my deepest core,
Just to remain where it is,
And never really be shown—to anyone.

Dark Days
How Many More?

How many miles does the wind flies?
How many clouds are there in the skies?
How many minutes are there in my pains?
How many people in my dreams, and in my life?

How many more days are to run through my fingers like soft, warm sand?... So much sand in my dunes, almost as much sun in my wishes... so many wishes that do not want to die, and so they desperately try to anchor themselves in the lightest memory of the shiniest sun, that once a year, with no exception they visit, making times sweeter and reinventing the best medicine for the unsaid words.

Almost as many shores in my seas, as many sailing ships in my days, like mirages that barely stay seconds in my eyes to disappear back again in the deepest bottom of the ocean that supports them all... and then, then they are all gone...

How many shores, and seas, and ships in the long days that live along my ocean?

Is the forever horizon, the only thing that stays, tirelessly constant, continuously present and, as forever horizon, always unreachable, only being lightly touched by the glance that rises at dawn, before going back to the darkness of dusk, always searching for the next sunrise light, the incomparable brightness of the golden sand, reflecting the new horizon's shine, under the light of the new dawn... How many unexplored horizons?

With the blank paper always daring me; today is winding, my inspiration gone, somewhere far, far away from home. Somewhere the light sand does not get to touch me, or my glance, or my hands or my desolated dreams and decaying... somewhere very away from my heart and the smile that flies my white cottony clouds high, full of clean, blue skies... How many blank, daring papers can I accommodate to fill in, without light and without dreams?

Like me, my dreams barely rest, barely stand a chance to get to shine, no matter how much I look for them... They always hide in the darkest, lost corner, of the last kingdom of my poor, confused soul, never to be found, never to be embraced, never recovered, never to be alive in my eyes that wish for them, desires them as water is longed for by the dry and lonely desert... almost like life itself...

My dreams, they always strange and I cherish the nights when they let me have wings, those mornings to wake up enlightened, brighter, lighter... One day, I will be able to enjoy fully that aftertaste in bed, with a coffee and the eternal love I can't help but to keep waiting for, just to fall again, deep into them, but awake this time...

How many strange dreams speak the truth of the lost soul that keeps crusading the skies in search for more, brighter and closer horizons filled in with tangible love and a truly, happy existence?

How many more?
That is a question that,
Until the right moment arrives,
Nobody, not even me,
Will be able to answer.
Always on the search for better, happier,
And brighter horizons.

The Sweet Little Girl

Sweet little girl, you will always have a heart, that heart, that renews its vows almost daily,

Monthly when the moon is full and new,

With that smile, with that little beautiful face that resembles the soul,

With so much passion, that almost breaks the world, with your steps,

The glances of that, little sweet girl, that fill with cuddles the air that herself breathes, alone or matched,

Like that little girl, who the same way she feels, she lets others feel,

The same way she lets each soul that walks with her, feel the same,

That sweet girl that does not want hollow doubts,

I ask myself, *Where did that sweet little girl go?*

In which moment did she get lost?

That is now so difficult to find her once more,

That little girl, who with her own life upheld, that it was easier to begin rather to keep going, straight, without a change, and after yet another day,

Where could now be that little girl?

What has been of her?

Of that life, that smile,
That unfortunately stained day-by-day,
That brightened glare, with the eager flight of fancy that only happens when nothing is possessed, but everything can be done,
When it does not matter how many times everything breaks down, in pieces, to let that emptiness being converted in grandiose wholeness,
Once and over again,
What could have been of that child, that breaks everything that gets into her hands, only to stare fixed to the core of what once was sustained,
Only to find out if it can be sustained again, only successfully this time.
That little girl, always was, doubtless, a bright shining star to chase…

> To that sweet little girl that will never leave me,
> Please keep reminding me who I am,
> And where I am headed,
> Please do never let me forget
> Where from did my soul come.

Answer to the Shakespeare's Tragedy of Hamlet

Perhaps then we should stick to this temple of mortal coil whilst the beautiful light of life fuels it and takes on all the seas of trouble and thus also preserves the temple of our sleep and faces the dreams that come, for not all are arrows and not all are heartaches, for in our temples may we keep a heaven of sweet, sweet deaths and entire seas, of secret kisses, some ungiven, others long kept after they were given.

I do not wish to rid my beautiful mortal temple. I do not wish to pause form kissing, as I do not wish to pause the sweet heartaches from coming, for are precisely those heartaches that colour the immense, beautiful, blue sea with the grandness of a thousand stars, filling my humble temple with the reflection of those dreams that one day, and every day I wish to be alive with.

And thus, I have decided to stay and face the seas of weak trouble for as long as my arms can stand and for as many stings and as many arrows they can oppose.

> Because nobody ever said it was going to be easy,
> Because it is infinitely worth it,
> And because, in spite all,

We cannot walk the streets like open wounds,
And not expect to find the right match
For our very long, ingrown dreams.

Never Coming Back

This is absolutely sick… being in here for like forever without noticing how the time… just goes… the way it slips away from my fingers like the handful of sand I try to keep in my half-closed fist… Meanwhile, nothing happens… no life but daily waking to nothing and loneliness, one day after another, just falling into slumber, so very much alone that my skin barely recognises the heart that keeps it alive, with a bed of sorrows, all to myself, just eat the air, just drink the tears, on my own… and a black hole, with a bunch of nothing that does not give a damn if I am alive or dead…

And just one day, all of a sudden, one wakes up tired and depressed, not wanting to go anywhere, not wanting to see anybody, enraged with the world and sick of being lonely, exhausted of living a life of isolation and sorrow, a life of darkness, rain and clouds…

And thus, one day, sanity issues start coming up out of the blue… only they did not actually come up out of the blue; there were very good reasons for them to get to where they did. They have simply been forming on the background along all the time spent crying tears of blood, angry at everything and everyone around, looking at the hours come and go, enclosed in the four walls that jail my spirit without anyone to share a hug with, no one to share a feeling, a fear,... just keeping everything inside... keeping it until it starts rotting, savagely enveloping one in disgust and rage, that ferocious, empty fear and other nasty feelings that eat you from inside out.

I pray to the universe I never have to come back to this hollow place, and utterly dark, of my life again, this lonely, discriminative, unfair space, this damn isolating place ever again... and I hope for the very sake of the sanity long ago lost, not knowing if ever is going to come back to me, to not to miss it because heavens know the way human being is; once you forget the wrongs, the poor, bare, little goods come forward, one just remembers those utterly bare goods, then everything seems to have happened in a very different way, and then one misses and wants to come back to its own jailor, its own doom...

So, I sincerely hope to very well remember the shadows, the precarious bridges I was obliged to build, quickly, in a desperate hurry... the way in which I have seen myself on the edge, the way I had to literally invent, out of nowhere, a new tool, a new secret shine, just in my mind to keep me going, to reach a safe shore, so, so much alone, so in the absolute dark that I had to actually stretch my hands to myself to know who I was, to talk to all those shadows with the fake smile, to wake up every morning, to swallow all that dark and going through it and over it. And all that just to find a decent thing to do, to not to drawn, a decent thing to do, to fill my hours with something I thought I was going to enjoy, but on the contrary, only deepened me more in loneliness and the regret of the long time spent, all the long alone years of my life which I could have spent, perhaps more wisely, doing almost anything else, may be more fulfilling, truly needed, now that I know. I would say, just being surrounded by people, I may have, in all this time even become important to someone, I could have been loved and appreciated by true smile with the right spirit.

I have only been alone instead... alone, forgotten and drinking the sorrows in the worst way, drinking my health in a hollow, solitary room, just wishing for something good to happen to me or even, simply around me, wishing for some tender, sincere hands to share my thoughts and rest my wishes on, to go dancing along and release some of that dark out of the unforgiving, restraining flesh... wishing, wishing, wishing,... just wishing, on my own...

Undergoing darker days than the nights themselves, darker thoughts than the deepest bottom of the deepest ocean... literally dragging the soul around, trying to clear the tears of my eyes whilst every morning walking towards nowhere, towards nothing, that cut the very roots of every possible happiness in me, every smile, every possible cool in me...

Rage aside, I have finally opened my eyes, finally realised that empty skin of nothing in this damn land is, and faces the same emptiness as me, uncaring, cold, shady, filled only with own interest and no more than that...

I have finally realised how fake every smile is, that will never find a hug in this darkness, never a true hand, that will never have a spirit to prompt the hearts to beat... I have finally realised now that I cannot live my life the way they do, in this obtuse, dark place, with no real smiles, with no spirit and with no colour.

And so, I find myself very, very much regretting not having awaking before, not having noticed all this before, in my own push for development, for more, for better, for more real and more feelings... Now I know I could have escaped this hell way before all the sanity issues where even preparing to come to me, for not having noticed, way before and used the precious time the way it deserves to be spent, and live a real life and start my days with a full heart, heading to brighter days filled with loving sun and true smiles that fill the spirits of my heart, getting to all my nights with a new wish to water my green feet on the ground and watch their rapid growth, the greenest and full of flowers new ground; I could have stared at the stars with the truest, steadiest peace in my heart, which is what all my existence is literally shouting for.

> At this very moment, sadly
> Only my own me and
> My stardust spirit.

A Day with My Dearest Nobody

Empty—nobody told me once he was feeling completely empty of everything. After all his hard work and all the efforts along his life, he was completely unable to find the way, he was unable to see it, to be confident that it was there, somewhere, to even know there were a way...

He also confided me that all this time has just helped him to keep going without life quality, sometimes, even without the very basic needs a complex being like him may have, and how all this started drowning his hopes, his strength, that his dreams were, day by day, just drifting away in that deep emptiness...

Suddenly, all the opportunities in front of him, just a step away, right there to take them, to make them his at once, to enjoy them to grow them, to fill in his days... just disappeared, leaving nothing behind but the vague memory of what could have been, leaving vague memories of how beautiful would have felt... but instead, just the emptiness...

He always used to ask himself what was the damn turn of this life that made him stop once and over again just in the edge of fulfilling the goals, what made him stop once and over again and turn back right before actually grasping the sweet victory that so hard he kept on working for? Could that be the stubborn destiny on the way, the stars telling him those victories, despite all, were not his to own? I remember this used to drag him crazy, and so many times drove him to be so close to quitting the game altogether... Thanks heavens, he did not.

But I know very well, even if he does not talk about this much, I know that some little stich remains in his heart even deeper, like a heavy weight he cannot be rid of and so the only thing left for him to do is just to hide it and keep carrying it in silence, as if it was a shame to be so unfairly mutilated by the moods and whims of this life, as if it was a sin to feel so deeply and being able to see what others did not even know it existed, as if the loneliness was the lame price to the utter greatness he, only sometimes, was aware he possessed.

He kept on asking himself why his needs would never be fulfilled. It wasn't like all of them were so complicated to be realized. One of those easy, uncomplicated needs was the learning of the very basic language he needed to speak in order to communicate with the fellow spirits around him, and nothing, no one, not a soul helped him to start speaking, and so, more than once he felt those words dying in his chest, tearing him apart like the furious, burning madness of the 'non-reason at all', those words that every time they were omitted, imploded in the depths of his consciousness, those unsaid words, unintentionally, turned into tears, and the tears turned into the very name of those unsaid words, just like that, like in a poem, or a tragedy.

And very much like in a poem or in a tragedy, he noticed he could not help to cry from time to time. He used to tell me that those tears, where the magic, unnamed names of those words he was unable to speak and he could not. He just did not know, for the life of him, how to let them out of his lips, so they could be properly shared, the way they deserved to be. No matter how imperious the need, he did not know to speak the language.

In his heart, he always knew he needed much more than that, but he also was sure that without that beginning, he was not going to make it, without that proper beginning he wasn't going to get to the destination; after all, that was the only reason he took that train for, and now every effort seemed to have been for nothing, like the emptiness we talked about before, dark and deep and painful like not knowing where we are... It was even worse for him. He did not even know who he was with. He started seriously doubting he was accompanied at all, by anyone else apart from the stars this is... It did not seem so... not to him...

He kept on telling me that his real desires were not to be rich or to own a castle in each beautiful country of this tired, worn off Earth. But those words, seemed somehow to have a double depth, not easily detectable at a first glance. I, somehow, simply knew he guarded the secret desire to travel far, far away where nobody knew him, and nobody could ever give their overwhelming and useless opinion of anything about him, of why his heart hurt that way, of why he loved wild life more than his own kind, of why he loved getting lost on the absolutely stunning blanket of stars that warmed the seas every summer. I always knew he was actually missing all the freedom of the wilderness, all that adventures this cruel world took from him. But he chose to hide from me too. He just focused on his real desire, to simply achieve in life everything he was capable of, and that was fairly understandable; he wanted to feel happiness, to feel satisfied after all his struggles and doings, all the hard work, about all the hours against his will, only to get to the part he was actually fighting for; he has planted a tree, he used to tell me, and now he wanted to enjoy under its safe cover and eat the sweet fruits all that carrying water and caring for it, have finally produced, but he never felt he could do so... He never even felt the tree growing or giving any fruit at all... He could only see the emptiness and feel those unsaid words burning his insides like fire...

I saw him losing confidence in himself. I saw him struggle where he used to shine. I saw him going down and gradually isolating himself, letting that fire grow inside him, where the tree should have been instead... I saw him painfully losing ground and the will to fight for it... and I could not help but understanding his loneliness and sorrow... his deepest rage before the hollow answer of this world had to offer him... just emptiness and that growing fire that was consuming everything that once lived in him...

It became clear my dearest nobody was, day by day, letting go, losing the grasp of all his expectations, letting them fall into that deep, dark hole where all his hopes were falling too. He always had this natural predisposition to work, harder and harder, no matter what, to get to taste that promised sweet fruit, that never get to his hands because, as he said, he couldn't find it. He never found even himself on the level he dreamt of. He continuously asked himself if that was the way, if there were any other ways? If, perhaps, there was no way at all?

Nobody kept on trying to make sense of it all, to explain himself but not finding the words, dying in each one of them, each time he tried to pronounce them; he was thirsty, lost for achievement, desperate to have something better, something that really warmed him and taught him to finally speak them and let them forever go, finally away from his chest, finally carrying the dark sorrows away with them.

Nobody just needed to have fresh start, a warmed heart, and a real kiss where to rest his true smile and look forward to that summer, full of blankets of stars, with his beloved, most beautiful ever glance, that only talked about sincere, immense, most soothing love…

To my dearest nobody,
Never despair, and always hope,
For far better and warmer to come,
Find your way to that eternal summer,
And that true love.

A Little Story

When all this started, May was less than year old. She wasn't even born yet actually... but nonetheless, she could remember one image, just one clear image; her father was angry. He was pacing up and down along the kitchen, while her mum pressed gently her back to the kitchen wall and sat down on the floor, covering her womb with her folded legs, her knees under her chin, secured by her arms, that she locked around them.

May was all a question herself, 'What is going on here? Why my father is so angry?' One question that only time would answer, not at once, like with a proper answer, but along what could count as many years of learning about her father and his senseless, brutal tantrums. That memory did not even go back to her until she was much, much older, like when you unbox all the pieces of a puzzle, and it does not come together, to be an image until you work it through, piece by piece. The memory was there; it just needed to be called back, unfolded, just needed a motive to open back to her and form the whole image before May's eyes.

A little while after that, May was born into this cold world, which she did not know yet, but she was just about to discover; there is very little or nothing she could remember since then. She remained oblivious to what happened from her birthday on. Until she was one and a half years old, then, her father decided that May, as woman to be, must wear earrings and so she must get the earrings holes; this had to happen the sooner, the better because, being a woman was synonym of suffering and vice versa... No?

Now May remembers again... a strange medical-puzzle table was half way into the corridor of her grandparents' flat, and May was laid down on it, God! That was cold. It was so damn cold... It was confusing. It was simply so different from the warmth and tenderness of her loving mother arms... May was scared and cried without end like an infant snatched out of the comfort and sweet cares that her mum was very careful to give to her first, beloved offspring day and night. The worst was that she did not know, once more, what was happening, why mum was not there and why that table was so awfully cold.

Everyone else was there though, around her, while she was laying in that stupid table, but, this time, despite her efforts to get them to reach for her, no one did, they just looked at her. A strange man with a white dressing gown suddenly stretched his arms towards May. Then she drifted away. She just wasn't any more in that table. She could not see all the family around her any more, nor what stranger was doing to her. May did not know then, but she escaped her little body that went on crying somewhere in the flat while her consciousness went after her mother.

Mia, May's mum, was a young, very clever and successful woman, only darkened by her egoistic, sexist and foolish husband—May's dad.

Mia was not too far away. In fact she left the corridor where her daughter was crying and, with both hands covering her ears, went straight to the only part of the flat where she was sure she couldn't hear her little one's desperate cries, to the balcony.

Mia did not know, maybe she never knew; May's mum was not going to be very long with her child, but none of them did know this yet. None of them knew they were not going to have the chance speak about these things, to have these types of conversations, destiny would not let them.

And May was, once more, next to Mia looking at her, her mum was sat in the floor again, with her back to the wall, only this time she was covering her ears as if the entire world was crumbling down and the noise was unbearable. May could feel her mother's suffering, her desperation. It was a very strange experience, as if she was inside her mother's thought, but she was still being her, it was just, her consciousness. May remembers all this but not the holes in her little ears being done, how that artefact drilled the soft skin of her lobes. The very moment that stranger stretched his arms to her, puff she was gone somewhere near her Mia.

They were, once more, two people in one, just like before being born... Although it was a stressful situation, it certainly felt way better than the cold table back in the corridor.

After this, there were no more moments like this one, no more travelling through the consciousness to reach to Mia's distress and escape from her own.

May will always remember and cherish these two memories like the invisible water that sustained her own being, like the light, the purest light that chased away all her darkness and fear. It was much easier then, when she had her mother's arms around her most of the time.

There were a lot to bear along the next years, and even beyond, when it only got worse.

The day Mia left her forever was the darkest ever times for May. The darkest, only some years after that, did May have very special night when the tender light of her mother was present, for one brief night, one ethereal dream, in which she could hug her again. But that is another story, quite different and distant like all the vague memories in which May guard her precious mum…

To May and Mia,
Who will always be together,
But never again will be able to hug each other.
Their love and the memories,
Is the only thing that will never die?
They both know this a little too well.

Want to Be Friends?

How artificial it is to feel better after a couple of beers. This is very common nowadays, though...

Today, I find myself short for feelings and all about tears... for no reason really... silly. Just maybe because of the dreams, so very deep and meaningful dreams, lately I dream much about animals, pets that are to pets, but stray animals, like cats and dogs. Sometimes I dream about people too. The latter are always present in much less pleasant dreams. I have always preferred animals than people that is nothing new.

The people I dream about are supposed friends, I say 'supposed' because I do not really recognise their faces and besides, who knows what that word really means 'friends'? Not many, that much I do know for sure.

The only friends of whom I enjoy the company, are the readings, the music I listen to and, from time to time, the dreams...

I use to dream with the day I finally find someone special, someone, willing to hold my glance into his eyes, for the rest of my life, forever...

Does he exist? Do they exist? Does anybody know what being a friend means? Perhaps I'll never know the answer of any of these questions.

Sometimes I feel stalked, like spied on, as if under the stare of the stupid owls that never rest and never cease to chase me; right under the vigilant look of those who have no wings, and even if they had them, they had long forgotten how to fly, those who are nowhere near being the pure souls of the creatures that are free and loving... nowhere near it.

I am starting feeling these little things in people and even in myself; these little things that I wasn't able to distinguish never before, their short and stupid pretending, like an empty play.

There are many types of people, the best ones though, are those who... once we open the door, and in many occasions, even long after having closed it, what really matters keeps flowing, back and forth between us.

So, we could ask ourselves, how many of those wonderful people have we met along our lives? How many miles have we walked along with them? How many times did we close the door for them? And, more importantly, how many times did we open it again?

May be more than enough times to tell us they are the right people to have close by, even when they are far. It would be then just our own fault if we do not pay enough attention or we do not look in the right direction...

So many times, even when one knows things, there is the need of hearing them out loud from somebody else before being completely able to face the reality—plainly. Not simple, but rough and intricate most of the times, like the awful being we end up being converted into, also, most of the times.

It is certainly not easy at all to get to them nor going through all these realisations and amendments. No, it is extremely hard and it feels very lonely to stand solo before everybody and everything else, feeling naked and unprotected, feeling vulnerable… It takes a lot of courage.

The courage to live out loud… the courage to live the whole life, fully, entirely, with all the loves and all they take away from you, with all the tears and all the laughter, even when they happen in the solitude of your room, with no one to share them with, like all the alone holidays, like all the thoughts that live and die in my restless mind.

Ahh… thoughts, all those thoughts, those good companions… When are people going to get to the beautiful realisation that, before anything else, we need to take our sweet time to properly allow the thoughts to be born, to mature, before finally they perfect, and then they sharp themselves before they can get to our lips, and only then to become the most beautiful words, and the most beautifully weighted, that hopefully one day we are not going to regret to have released into the open.

Everything is a process, they say, even life is a process, no?

In any other occasions when I did not follow this process, I ended up regretting, very much regretting whatever I did or say. I have found myself regretting sometimes even allowing myself and others to certain glances.

The only thing I have never regretted is the music, not around and not into my deepest existence, not now, not ever. They say music calms the beasts, and I should hold that as true, because I have felt it. I have felt how the music lets the rage slowly fall asleep and disappear, and go away… almost forever…

To those friends that never were,
To those friends that have always been,
Those who always stood by me,
Even through the utter physical distance,
That makes everything fade into desolation.
To all those who never gave up, and always waited for me
To be ready to come back home.
To all of them, I truly thank you.

Never Ever Age

I live a life full of incomplete diaries, most of the times not even properly started diaries. May be that reason why I look so young despite all that is inside? Or maybe because I dance at each chance I get? Perhaps is because I dance alone, a lot?

Perhaps the reason is mi regular, nocturnal trips to other far away worlds, where I feel more like myself, I feel whole, and infinitely more secure... May be the reason why do not age is because I do not watch the news, but the thing, I just do not feel my age on me, I can't find the way to completely mature, I can't find it, and I do not want to, not today, not ever.

I want to be free; I want to be forever the child with the deep, intense glance and bright, sweet that does not notice the way life goes, the way it slips like the time that disappears before one can even see it coming. I want to be that child that never stops dancing in a corner of her heart, playing to be a grownup, wearing her mum's hills, filling her heart of magical lights, switching them on in the middle of the summer, the Christmas lights in her bedroom, just for her... because even when it does make sense, it does for her...

I might even be my way to see things, to contemplate them, so free, so rare, so mine, my way... I can always see the jewel hiding in each one of the nooks of this life, around each corner, wherever I go, there is always a light that stares at me from behind all the fog that separates us... I always find a guide... always something that makes me feel enough and does not let me age...

I always find a white piece of paper to fill in with the ink of my hopeful pen, that life has given me, together with another morning, one more day... to dance perhaps... but never to age...

Perhaps it is all the love I find in the universe, and how similar are its stars to the moles in my skin, even the beauty ones, those that draw constellations in it. I find it terribly funny and special, as if the universe seeks to tell me something important, and it does not want me to forget it...

It is not just my imagination. I find it in every fibre of my body, in each one of my thoughts, in each moment of rage and in each pleasant day... Even when I hurry, I always take my sweet time, always, to ask my grandest companion everything I need to know... to keep my childhood going on...

Who knows, perhaps I don't age because I am still learning yet, and growing, but only in the inside, only in the good way, may be because I always try not to take the life's lessons very seriously... and I always keep the good girl hiding, driving the ship from the deepest place of her soul, but always allowing the bad girl to give the orders to the crew...

And this way, letting the ship dance the rock of the sweet waters of the five oceans and their biggest waves, the most brutally sincere, truest waves... This is the way in which this wonderful life of which we are part of, is lived properly, with no fear to the future, despite the pain of yesterdays, and excited to know what is coming tomorrow, and if it will be the way I have always imagined it, the way I have always dreamt it would be, becoming even younger every day.

Life is funny like that, almost like me, almost like all those I have encountered, like all those that kiss me the first time we meet, and those who never do, either way, I notice they are all scared, and this is why they all go away right after kissing me for the first time, and even when they don't. I still don't know if it's because of me, or maybe they just don't know what to do with so much magic, so much dark and light…

May be the wholeness given step by step, the deep pain of the forever lost hug, and the bravery of waking up every day, and stand again, pushing oneself… to the infinite… and beyond, if need be, to never, ever age.

It might be the grandness of the whole universe inside me, that every day and every occasion takes its time to teach me, to make me just a little bigger, just a little older even when I cannot see it, because I am unable to. I am never able to see things in me… not even the hurriedly escaping time…

It is not just my imagination; I am so alive that I can feel the rivers of the Earth running through my veins, and the dawns of my thoughts filling the horizon…

Just one more reason to be alive, to breath the freedom… Is, just one more reason why I do not age…

> Never ever age,
> Never tire of being alive,
> Always feel the freedom
> And magnificence of the rivers of this Earth
> Running through your veins,
> Always live to the fullest, always dance.

My Beautiful Moon and Its Gifts

I love it when the moon comes to visit me, to call me through my window, like a bandit lover, and takes me out of my lethargy. She takes me out of my tired, exposed agony in front of a computer boring and quiet, just like me.

When the moon comes, ahh... when the moon comes, to throw pebbles to my window, peeking out between the clouds, that do not dare to hold her back, when she comes to shout mi name in a very low, sweet voice, so low voice that only my spirit can hear her, right before my eyes look in her direction to see her absolutely brilliant, clean shine, almost blue, like her wonderful night...

When the precious moon takes me out of my lethargy, there is a whole party happening in my soul that flies to the infinite to take a walk with her, staring to her eyes, along those blue streets of invisible winds, this is how I love the beloved lover of my dreams, this is how I feel her...

When she takes me wandering the world along through those seas of peace, when she has a glass of wine with me on the shores of the immense dusk, when she lays me down on the cool sand is when she is the only light, and the stars her beauty moles, that beautifully draw the bluest of her precious, ethereal body, of eternal magic... on our clearest, wide sky...

Ahh... my beautiful moon, I would like to live with you in the shores of our sweetest summer, and the longest one, those sweet summers of salty waters and clear like a blessing, the summers of tranquil tides that soften the days while I wait for you with my infinite, laying down on the same shores, under the sun...

This is how I love my moon, lover, bandit and adventurous, always daring, always fresh and full of life, always sleeping during the day and always dancing the nights with her beauty moles that only gift mysticism to her beautiful face...

This is how I wait every night for my beloved lover to take me away, to dance the world along the tides, the seas and all the shores where we rest before the sun comes... and we go to dance again...

> To my beautiful moon,
> Which is always my favourite lover,
> And the truest.

Something Different

It is well known and almost a fact that we should never judge a book by its cover, nor blindly choose it by its title. This being said, it is also true that some titles just catch you; they call your eyes, almost naming them, only to fill them with curiosity for knowing more about all the awesome words and unbelievable stories they guard inside the book that keeps them all together, but even though you just do not want to believe that very first impression you get, and so you push yourself, you go a little deeper, reading the bit at the back of the publication, and there you go, then you really start getting a real first impression is only then when you really start feeling something...

Something, but still not quite enough, still not enough to decide, and you go further (Always go further, only if in any way you value your own opinion and do not want to fail in one of the most important decisions you will ever make.), so you go for some more finding out, and pondering before you rush into this decision making...

You finally open that book (which, anyways, it results to be just an extension, or maybe a sincere explanation of your own life, it does not even matter the type of adventure, love story, or tragedy it talks about), the first pages seem to be a fine space where to find out could be just provable, I've always questioned though, the reasons why they misuse that very first page to leave in blank, when it could be filled out with fantastic turns of the story I am 'bout to read, I believe, there is simply, no explanation for that...

It does not get any better in the 'acknowledgements' page, the editorial stuff and so on... although in between so much preamble, sometimes, one can find a bit of something interesting that may be named prologue or something like that...

You pass all those empty pages and almost desperately look for the first chapter, the title, the first words... If you don't keep close track of the time and yourself in that moment, many times you would be able to read the entire book there and then... Those are the books that one ends up taking home, to devour them as if there were not tomorrow... as if they were water and you were I the middle of the desert... those, are real drops of light...

In the end, a book is just a reflection of a lonely soul, although one capable, of showing to the world what it is made of and giving them the exceptionally alive opportunity to escape their cruel reality for some time, beyond their physical eyes, beyond their physical being...

Personally, when it comes to books and me... how to explain it... the wildest thoughts fill my mind and me... entirely and almost savagely when I am in front of my little private library. I could never change it for anything in this world. They were my very careful choice. They hold my purest feelings and a very important prat of my life, very important moments of it...

Someone once tried to convince me to give them away, so others can read them too... 'I don't know about that,' I said, 'after having them in my hands, for as long as they had me feeling them, for as long as they have filled me with themselves, with so much intensity that I could almost touch it...' The sole thought of it gave me this weird cold chill, this unpleasant chill in my spine... unthinkable... 'It would be like giving away one of your own best friends,' I said. 'I could never do such a thing, and if I did it, I would never forget. I would end up buying them again, the same ones, once over... just to have them...'

Giving your book away seems indeed like giving your own best friend to some people about whom you do not know anything really... like giving them up to nothing, like burning them, the same way the sole thought of it burns myself from the inside out... I could never do such a thing... A wise man once said,

'If you care for a book, never ever lend it.'

I entirely praise and stick to that.

To my beautiful, little library,
Because it is my precious little collection,
One of the most beautiful things I have ever felt,
They are the closest kisses,
And they guard some of the
Most cherished moments of my life,
The moments I have spent with each one of those books on my hands.

Sandalwood

When the sandalwood of my thoughts rains over me, when it rains over my darkest and lightest dreams, they seem to catch the strength to fill the horizon with new and brighter stars, by the hand of the biggest and brightest moon, that never ceases to love me, as nor me to loving her back, the moon that sings in my ear, those special lullabies to heal the wounds, the deepest stiches, to take me out, once more for that unique dance of hers, that leads the mind of the prancing heart to the soothing, musical silence of the night...

When the sandalwood sings with the moon, to fill the darkest room in the world with her infinitely, lightest light of all, when they light the softest incense that fills the same darkest room with airs of many other places of the world, places that I have been, those places that perhaps one day I will visit...

When the moon and her sandalwood sing to me... is just amazing the way it feels, and it is only comparable to the way it feels the dragging of my pen over the virgin field, to leave this sentiment forever with it, and take with me, just a little part of it...

Each time I travel, I buy a notebook, different notebooks with different types of paper, completely white, gridded, smooth or rough, yellowy when it is recycled, they are all of them unique fields, but with the same sandalwood spirit, that awaits to have the longed romance with my pen in the presence of my incense and my moon... They will get their moment of glory, and then they will live tirelessly in the heavens of a little story, of some shared tears with the world that wants to read them, they will live with all the light and all the dark I have to give them.

Sandalwood... is like the thin, personal scent of this old house, like the way the sun rises over it. I guess it is the personal signature of this town, so big, so full of people, so full of everything, and so empty of what really matters in life...

This old house, I don't know why I don't spend more time in the kitchen, it may be best and the only way to socialise in this dark mass of hollow humans and, as difficult as it may be, finally find myself somewhere in it, perhaps I did not realise that, or perhaps I really don't care much for anyone in this house or in this town for that matter... perhaps so many hours craving to feel the sun on my skin have changed me so badly that I do not even get to recognise myself anymore...

When I try to ask to the moon but she's already gone, the gentle magic of the candles she lit before, their gentle light, and gentle touch, keeps our gobble alive, while I fight back the reckless Vikings' attacks, until she comes back to me, dancing her way, to take me once over to the stars, to spend the night together...

The songs of the moon and the sandalwood are the only things I care to take with me when I am gone, absolutely nothing more...

To my favourite sandalwood incense,
Because I absolutely love the way in which
It soothes my soul and makes me see things
In a different light. It really lights my loneliest nights.

Made in the USA
Monee, IL
03 May 2026

49437984R00036